THE CRYSTAL BEADS
LALKA'S JOURNEY

BY PAT BLACK-GOULD

ILLUSTRATIONS BY
KATYA ROYZ

Purple Butterfly Press
An Imprint of Kat Biggie Press
Columbia, SC

Published by Purple Butterfly Press, 2022
Columbia, South Carolina
info@purplebutterflypress.net

The text of this book is adapted from the short story, *The Crystal Beads,* that was previously published in Jewish Fiction .net.

Illustrator: Katya Royz

Designer: Sunny Duran

Editor: Caroline Smith, Dakota Nyght

Library of Congress Control Number: 2021913962

PRINTED IN THE UNITED STATES OF AMERICA

Publisher's Cataloging-In-Publication Data
(Prepared by The Donohue Group, Inc.)

Names: Black-Gould, Patricia, author. | Royz, Katya, illustrator.
Title: The crystal beads : Lalka's journey / written by Patricia Black-Gould ;
   illustrations by Katya Royz.
Description: [Columbia, South Carolina] : Purple Butterfly Press, 2022. |
   Interest grade level: K-3. | Summary: "A Star of David or a rosary? In
   1939 Poland, a young Jewish girl must reject one of these and accept
   the other without understanding why. The girl's mother is forced to
   make a heartbreaking sacrifice to keep her daughter safe"-- Provided by publisher.
Identifiers: ISBN 9781955119207 (hardcover) | ISBN 9781955119214
   (paperback) | ISBN 9781955119221 (ebook)
Subjects: LCSH: Jewish children in the Holocaust--Poland--History--20th
   century--Juvenile fiction. | Mothers and daughters--Poland--History--
   20th century--Juvenile fiction. | Judaism--Juvenile fiction. | Catholic
   Church--Juvenile fiction. | CYAC: Jewish children in the Holocaust--
   Poland--History--20th century--Fiction. | Mothers and daughters--
   Poland--History--20th century--Fiction. | Judaism--Fiction. | Catholic Church--Fiction.
Classification: LCC PZ7.1.B5664 Cr 2022 (print) | LCC PZ7.1.B5664
   (ebook) | DDC [E]--dc23

For the children —
Those who perished and those who survived
May they live forever in our hearts

To my husband —
Who was a source of support and encouragement
throughout the writing of this book

***

How wonderful it is that nobody need wait a single moment
before starting to improve the world.

— Anne Frank

Poland 1939

On my seventh birthday, Mama bought me a beautiful necklace.

"This is a special present," she said as she held up crystal beads that sparkled when touched by the sunlight streaming through our apartment's kitchen window.

My fingers grasped the gold Star of David I wore around my neck every day. "It's so pretty, Mama, but I always wear the necklace Papa gave me."

"This is not a necklace, my Lalka." I liked when Mama called me Lalka, her doll. But dolls were little, and I was a big girl. She placed the crystals in my hand, and I held them up. The summer sunlight kissed the beads, making rainbow dots that danced on our lemon-yellow kitchen walls.

"If it's not a necklace, Mama, what is it?"

"It's called a rosary, Lalka. Can you say that word?"

"Rose-a-ree."

"Very good. Now, I'd like to teach you a special game. This rosary is part of it. Are you ready to learn?"

"Oh, yes!" I loved playing games with my mother.

"See the cross on the bottom? That is called a crucifix. Can you say that word?"

"Cru-sa-fix," I said, but the figure on the cross frightened me, so I didn't touch that part.

"You are so smart." Mama ruffled my hair. "But it is important that you listen carefully. You need to take this rosary with you everywhere you go. Do you understand?"

"So I should keep this with me, like I wear Papa's necklace every day?"

"No, Lalka. An important part of this game is that I give you this rosary in exchange for your necklace."

"But Papa told me the necklace was special. He said the shape of the six-pointed star looked like King David's shield and it would protect me." Besides, my father gave me the Star of David on my fifth birthday, just before he died, and I wanted to keep it.

My mother placed an open, shaky hand on the white lace tablecloth. "You must trust me, Lalka." I thought I saw tears in her eyes. Maybe she was thinking of Papa.

When I handed my mother the necklace, she held it to her heart. "I promise to keep this safe," she said and then placed it in her dress pocket. "It's time to teach you more of the game."

For the next few months, Mama showed me books with pictures of angels and crosses on the covers. And she taught me that each crystal bead on the rosary had its own prayer. Alone in my bedroom at night, I practiced the prayers over and over.

Then one day, a woman who lived in the neighborhood visited us. She told stories about Jesus and the saints and taught us songs. My mother and I sang so much our throats ached.

Early one cold winter morning, Mama told me we were taking a trip. She had packed a bag. It was the one we used when Papa took us on vacation a long time ago.

"Are we going to the lake?" I asked.

"Oh, if only we could. Today, we are doing something different. You are going to learn the most important part of the game."

"I know a lot already, don't I?"

"Yes, that's why you're ready for this trip." She helped me put on my heavy coat. "Oh, wait." She rushed into her bedroom and came back with a blue wool scarf she had just finished knitting. In her other hand, she held an almost empty bottle of lavender perfume that Papa gave her a long time ago.

When I was little, Mama always wore the lavender scent, and I loved cuddling with her and breathing in the fragrance. But no stores carried perfume anymore.

She laid the scarf on the kitchen table and sprinkled the few remaining drops of lavender on the wool. Then she wrapped the scarf around my neck. "You will always have this memory."

Mama carried the suitcase and held my hand as we headed down the stairs and into the street. We walked for a long time and my legs hurt. At the edge of town, she stopped in front of a tall, dark building with a tower.

"There's a cross in the sky," I said.

"Yes. It's on top of the church steeple."

We climbed the stone steps, and my mother opened the heavy wooden door. My eyes had to adjust to the dim light. Holding hands, we headed down a long aisle between wooden benches. At the end, I noticed a large marble cross hanging on the center wall and ran toward it. "Look, Mama, this one's a cru… crucifix!"

"That's correct," a voice spoke from behind me.

I turned around and looked up at a woman wearing a long black robe. Stiff white fabric framed her face, and I wondered if the material was itchy. Once I had a stiff dress that itched when I sat down.

The woman smiled and extended a thin, wrinkled hand out of the wide black sleeve of her robe. "Hello, my child. I'm Sister Teresa. "

"She will help you learn the rest of the game," Mama said.

Sister crooked her finger. "Come, let me show you the church and the statues of the saints. I will teach you their names."

I pointed to one statue of a woman wearing a blue robe. "That one is Mary, Jesus' mother."

Sister nodded and spoke to Mama, "I see you've been teaching her."

My mother wrung her hands.

"Ah. I know," Sister said to me. "I'll teach you how to genuflect. This is something Catholics do when we enter a church. It's our way to praise God."

Genuflect. What a strange word.

Sister Teresa bent her right knee almost to the ground in a gentle and smooth movement and rose again.

My mother took my hand. "Let's do it together." We both bent our right knees. I had trouble balancing and bumped into Mama. We tumbled to the ground, and she scooped me in her arms. We laughed so hard tears ran down our cheeks.

When we stood, Mama touched my cheek. "Now comes the most important part of the game, Lalka. You must stay here with Sister for a while."

I grabbed Mama's coat. "Will you stay too?"

"I can't," she said. "But many children come to school here and live together."

My fingers dug into the wool, not letting go. "No, I want to go home!"

Mama removed an envelope from her purse and handed it to Sister Teresa. "These are all the papers. How can I thank you for this? I worry I'm placing you at risk."

Sister Teresa spoke in a soft voice. "I trust in God. I trust that the power that joins us is greater than anything that might divide us."

They shared a look I did not understand.

My mother hugged me. "I will come back as soon as I can." She held me tight as I breathed in the familiar scent of her perfume. "Promise me you will keep playing the game." Tears flowed down her cheeks as she backed away.

Through sobs, I could barely say the words, "I promise, Mama."

Sister Teresa put her arm around my shoulder. I sobbed as I watched my mother leave the church.

The children at the school all wore uniforms and Sister gave me one too. In my classroom, I learned as many prayers and songs as the other kids knew. We all went to Mass together in the big church. And we celebrated holidays I had never heard of before.

When my mother came to visit, we would always meet in Sister Teresa's office. I'd tell her about everything I had learned. Once I even showed her how to genuflect—the correct way. But she still tipped over and we both laughed.

Before each visit, Sister Teresa would come into to my classroom to get me. I'd race out of the room, and run down the hall to Sister's office, where my mother waited with open arms. But after a few weeks, Mama's visits stopped, and I would cry myself to sleep at night.

Sometimes, when I became sad, Sister took me into her office. She would tell me stories about her family and the Polish countryside where she grew up. On the corner of her desk, she kept a tall gold cross that I admired. She said her parents gave it to her as a present on the day she became a Bride of Christ.

I loved that cozy room. On bright days, the sun would shine through the large windows. I'd hold up my crystal beads and watch the rainbow dots dance on the walls, just like they had done at home on my last birthday.

Then one day, Sister Teresa opened the door to our classroom. She glanced at me.

Mama's here! I raced out of the room.

"Wait," she called from down the hall. But I was moving too fast, ready to run into my mother's arms and smell her sweet lavender perfume.

When I opened the office door, Mama wasn't there. Instead, two men wearing long black leather coats and dark hats stood in front of the large window. Behind them, heavy rain fell outside. The wind howled, and the windowpanes rattled. I felt a chill and wrapped my arms around myself.

The men, one tall with dark eyes, and the other short, with a round red face, stared at me. I lowered my eyes and noticed the hems of their coats. Drops of water slinked like snakes down the leather. Small puddles formed on the wooden floor around their shoes.

I backed away, only to bump into Sister's desk, knocking over her gold cross.

Sister Teresa panted as she entered the room, then placed a hand on my shoulder. "These men want to speak to you."

I don't understand. Did I do something wrong?

The tall, dark-eyed man towered over Sister. In a stern voice, he told her to leave. Sister didn't move. Her hand gripped my shoulder so tight it hurt.

"We wish to speak to her alone," he said through a smile that quickly vanished.

After Sister left, the man closed the door. He shouted questions at me. I knew the answers because Mama had taught me.

But then the short, red-faced man spoke. "Do you understand what a sin is?"

My heart was pounding. "Sister Cecelia told us that if you commit a mortal sin, and don't confess it, you're condemned to the everlasting fires of Hell."

"So, you understand it's a sin if you don't tell the truth."

Oh, no. He knows what I did! "Uh, yes. I'm sorry I stole bread from Piotr. I was hungry and sometimes there's not much food. But it was only *one* piece. I promise to tell Father Emil in confession on Friday. May I please leave now?"

"Not yet." The short man dug something out of his pocket. Between his thick fingers, he held up a chain with a gold star dangling at the bottom. "Did you ever see this before?"

Papa's necklace! Why does he have it, Mama?

When I didn't answer, the man grunted. He threw the necklace on the floor as though getting rid of a piece of garbage. It landed in a puddle of rainwater near my feet.

I wanted to scoop it up and clutch it to my heart. Instead, I stepped away. But my legs trembled, and I had trouble standing, so I lowered myself to the floor.

The tall, dark-eyed man moved closer and hissed. "*You're* a filthy Jew. You should be wearing a yellow star, like the rest of them."

Mama, help me. What do I do?

For an instant, it was my seventh birthday again. There was Mama, speaking to me as she held up the crystal beads. "This is a special present," she said.

But her voice faded as the men shouted, "Jew, Jew, Jew."

I reached into my sweater pocket, fumbling for the rosary. Clasping it tightly in one hand, I made the sign of the cross and prayed. "In the name of the Father, the Son, and the Holy Ghost."

"Jew, Jew, Jew."

My hands gripped the crucifix, the image that had once frightened me. "Our Father, who art in heaven, hallowed be thy name. Thy kingdom come…"

Through my prayers, the men's voices boomed as they repeated those words.

I kept my eyes closed as tears streamed down my face. "Lead us not into temptation…" My voice grew louder. "But deliver us from evil…"

For a while their voices continued. Their boots clicking on the floor. Then the door slammed, and I cringed.

There was silence. Then someone grabbed my arm. I pulled away and crouched into a tiny ball on the floor, the crystal beads in my fist, still praying.

In a soft voice, I heard Sister speak, "They're gone, child." She wrapped her arms around my shaking body and rocked me. "You're safe now."

My eyes darted around the room as my fingers moved over the beads.

Sister Teresa held out her thin hand. In her palm was the Star of David.

Through my tears, I glanced at the crystal beads in my hand and the gold necklace in hers. "Sister," I asked. "Which one of these is the sin?"

Afterword

Children can make a difference, one class at a time

Years ago, I heard a story about a young Jewish girl who was sent to a convent during the Holocaust. The child survived, but her mother did not. I felt the need to record their story because I wondered how hatred could have the power to destroy millions of lives.

How could we teach compassion and caring so something like this would never happen again? That's when I discovered Whitwell Middle School, located in a small town in rural Tennessee. What happened in those classrooms changed the lives of the students and made an impact on the world.

In 1998, Principal Linda M. Hopper, Vice-Principal David Smith, and eighth-grade teacher Sandra Roberts wanted children to learn about empathy and respect for different cultures. So they designed a course to teach students about the Holocaust and the six million Jews who perished. Six million was a hard number for the students to comprehend! So Ms. Roberts and her class decided they needed to collect six million of something. But what? The students learned that during World War II, the people of Norway wore paper clips on their lapels to protest the Nazi occupation. They also found out that the paper clip was invented by a Norwegian Jew. For those reasons, they decided to collect paper clips, with each clip representing a life lost.

Due to the hard work of the students and teachers, donations came in from school children, Holocaust survivors, celebrities—even United States presidents! The school met its goal of six million paper clips, and then collected five million more, dedicating them to the five million others killed by the Nazis, including individuals with disabilities, gay people, priests, Jehovah's Witnesses, Roma people, and resistance fighters in occupied countries.

The school needed a place to store the paper clips. With the help of two White House correspondents, Whitwell staff and students obtained a German cattle car that Nazis had used to transport Jews to concentration camps, one of the few cars left from that era. Eleven million paper clips are stored in two glass cases situated on either end of the boxcar. As of the writing of this book, thirty-three million paper clips have been collected. Some of these clips have been distributed to other schools that have started their own paper clip projects.

The Children's Holocaust Memorial, located on the school campus, receives visitors from around the world. Students give tours to school groups and individuals who visit the museum. Ms. Roberts is retiring at the end of the 2022 school year, but her legacy will continue. Taylor Kilgore, a former Whitwell student, received her master's degree in Holocaust and Genocide Studies and will take over the program in the next school year.

How could such an amazing project happen in a small town? When I asked that question of Dr. Josh Holtcamp, the current school principal, he stated that Whitwell Middle School had already had a caring culture that allowed such a program to grow and flourish.

Now that you've read Lalka's story and have learned about Whitwell, think about how you can discover ways you can make a difference in the lives of others. Think about Anne Frank's quote at the beginning of this book: "How wonderful it is that nobody need wait a single moment before starting to improve the world."

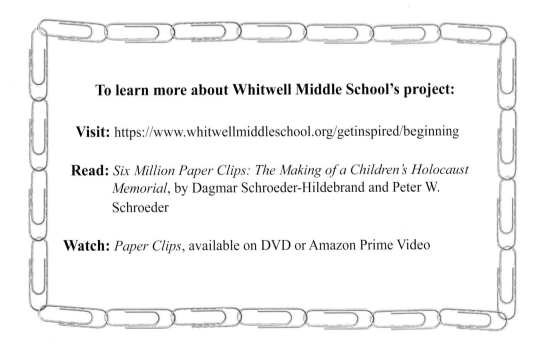

To learn more about Whitwell Middle School's project:

Visit: https://www.whitwellmiddleschool.org/getinspired/beginning

Read: *Six Million Paper Clips: The Making of a Children's Holocaust Memorial*, by Dagmar Schroeder-Hildebrand and Peter W. Schroeder

Watch: *Paper Clips*, available on DVD or Amazon Prime Video

Children's Study Guide Questions

1. Why didn't the little girl want to give up her Star of David, the necklace with the six-pointed star? What was the girl's response to the rosary?

2. Why do you think her mother made up the game and played it with her? What are examples of their game?

3. Why did the mother take the girl to the church and leave her with Sister Teresa? How do you think the girl felt? How do you think her mother felt? How would you feel if your mother had to leave you with someone you didn't know?

4. Why did the two men come to the school to speak to the girl? Why did they want to speak to her in private? How did the girl feel about the questions she was asked? How can you tell?

5. What do you suppose the little girl was thinking when she saw the man hold up the chain with the Star of David between his fingers? Why did he throw the necklace on the floor?

6. How do you think the men treated the girl? What did they say or do that frightened her? If you saw someone in your school treat another child in the same manner, would you say or do something about it?

7. The men told the little girl she needed to tell the truth. They said if she didn't tell the truth, she would be committing a sin. What did the men mean by this?

8. In this story, the six-pointed star and the rosary are symbols of two religions. If your family practices a religion, are there one or more symbols associated with it? If so, what do these symbols mean to you?

9. At the end of the story, after the men leave, Sister Teresa has the Star of David necklace in her hand and the girl holds the rosary in hers. Why does she ask the Sister which of them is the sin?

10. Throughout the story, the girl's mother calls her *Lalka,* which means "doll" in Polish. Why do you think the author chose not to give the girl a name?

Adult Study Guide Questions

1. In the story, Sister Teresa says to the mother, "I trust that the power that joins us is greater than anything that might divide us." What does she mean by this statement?

2. What role does faith play in this story?

3. Symbols have always played a dominant role in culture. In this story, what symbols do you identify and what are their meanings?

4. The men in the story tell the little girl that if she doesn't tell the truth, she is committing a sin. What makes something a sin? Is it a personal rule, a religion, a situation, or a state of mind? Does it vary from person to person or is it steadfast?

5. This story is told from a child's point of view. In what way does this point of view magnify the terrors of life under the Nazi regime?

6. Many people risked their lives to help Jews flee or go into hiding during World War II. Why would people put their lives at risk to protect others? Discuss other examples of self-sacrifice and courage.

7. In an age of disinformation and conspiracy theories, how do people choose who or what to believe? What leads people toward making those choices? How do people know which sources to trust?

8. Discuss how this story can help teach lessons of compassion, tolerance, and empathy. What are the consequences of not learning such lessons?

9. How might an individual's personal experiences impact their views of other races, belief systems, or cultures?

10. Given ongoing global conflicts, what is your opinion that another large-scale genocide could occur, not only to Jews but to other populations as well? Discuss other groups who have suffered, or are currently suffering, from human rights violations.

The Words of a Holocaust Survivor

When the war began, I was a little over three years old. Our family fled from the Jewish town of Derazhnya, and the Nazis followed us, literally 30 kilometers behind us. We took refuge in the woods or asked for asylum from local residents, and more often than not, we were refused. My parents explained to these people that they still had two houses in Derazhnya, but they left it all because they decided to save all of us children. In response, my parents heard, "Who made you embark on such a difficult path? You should have stayed there." But my parents knew that when the Nazis came, they would destroy everyone, which later happened to our numerous relatives and friends.

Fascist Germany set itself the goal of exterminating the Jews of Europe and the Soviet Union. It was an unprecedented phenomenon until now—the destruction of people just for their ethnicity and religious beliefs.

Our family are the survivors of the Holocaust. None of us, my parents and eight brothers and sisters, ever returned to Derazhnya, and we knew perfectly well that all the Jews who remained there were killed.

***

The Crystal Beads is a story about a rescued girl, written by Pat Black-Gould. The Holocaust should never be forgotten, and this story once again reminds us of these events. She talks about the sacrifices made and the hardships endured by parents in order to save their children. This is a story about kindness, mercy, and courage. She raises many important questions that need to be remembered so that this will never happen again.

Efim Royz, Katya Royz's grandfather
Honored Worker of Culture, musician
Honorary Citizen of the town of Mezhdurechensk, Siberia

The Words of a Holocaust Survivor's Son

In her lovely story, *The Crystal Beads*, Patricia Black-Gould recounts the journey of a Jewish child whose mother has to prepare her to become Catholic and place her in a convent in order to save her from the Nazis. It is a story all too familiar to survivors of the Holocaust and their children. I know this because similar events happened to people close to me.

Having taught the Holocaust to youngsters, I am aware of the challenges presented by the subject matter. Dr. Black-Gould's story introduces the reader to the Holocaust through the eyes of the little girl who has to exchange her treasured Star of David necklace for the crystal beads of a rosary. By not giving the little girl a name, the author allows the reader to understand and empathize with her. She is both every little girl who survived the Holocaust and every child who reads her story. The three characters, the mother, the child, and Sister Theresa, stare into the face of tragedy with great courage.

I firmly believe that parents and teachers should share the story of the Holocaust with their children and students. Like the story of Anne Frank, it is a story that must be told. Concerned parents often ask if children can handle the subject of the Holocaust. The answer is yes, if its story is told with subtlety and grace, as is true in *The Crystal Beads* and where the tragedy is redeemed by love.

Rabbi Mark W. Kiel
New York

About the Author

Pat Black-Gould, PhD, is a clinical psychologist and an author. Her short stories have appeared in several literary journals and anthologies. Many years ago, Pat heard a powerful story that haunted her until she committed it to paper. *The Crystal Beads* was first published in Jewish Fiction .net in 2020. The short story then won first-place honors in two writing competitions conducted by the National League of American Pen Women, Inc., Washington, D.C. The first was an award by the Florida State Association NLAPW, Inc. Pat then received the Flannery O'Connor Short Story Award as part of the National Biennial Letters Competition.

Pat felt it was important to bring the story to a younger audience. At that point, she rewrote it as a children's book. She hopes that *The Crystal Beads, Lalka's Journey* will do justice to the story she once heard and carry its message to younger generations.

Pat's writing explores topics such as compassion, tolerance, and diversity. She continues to examine these themes in her upcoming novel, *Limbo of the Moon*, written with her co-writer, Steve Hardiman. Pat has also published a book chapter and professional journal articles on Deaf studies and mental health with her co-author, Dr. Neil Glickman.

Author Photo by Nancy Nesvik

About the Illustrator

Ekaterina Royz is an artist, illustrator, and educator who teaches drawing to children and adults. Since 2017, she has lived in Israel, where she repatriated from Siberia. When Katya received a message from Pat with a proposal to illustrate *The Crystal Beads*, she had no doubt that this was exactly the kind of subject matter she felt passionate about. The events of World War II and the Holocaust personally affected Katya's family. Her grandfather, Efim Royz, was born in Ukraine, in the Jewish town of Derazhnya, into a large family: a mother, father, and nine children.

In the summer of 1941, Nazi troops occupied Derazhnya. The Royz family was one of the few who fled Derazhnya before the Nazis arrived. Numerous relatives and friends stayed there, hoping that everything would be okay. The Jewish ghetto was established in Derazhnya. On September 20 and 21, 1942, the German Sonderkommando shot the entire Jewish population of the city—more than 3,500 people.

Katya's great-grandfather, great-grandmother, and their children made it to Siberia despite great difficulties, and therefore everyone was saved. For Katya, the topic of the Holocaust is close to her heart and interesting not only because it is an important period in world history, but also because of her personal family history.

In addition to illustrating, Katya collaborates on educational projects on a wide variety of subjects, including the Holocaust, for young people in Israel, Russia, and the Commonwealth of Independent States.